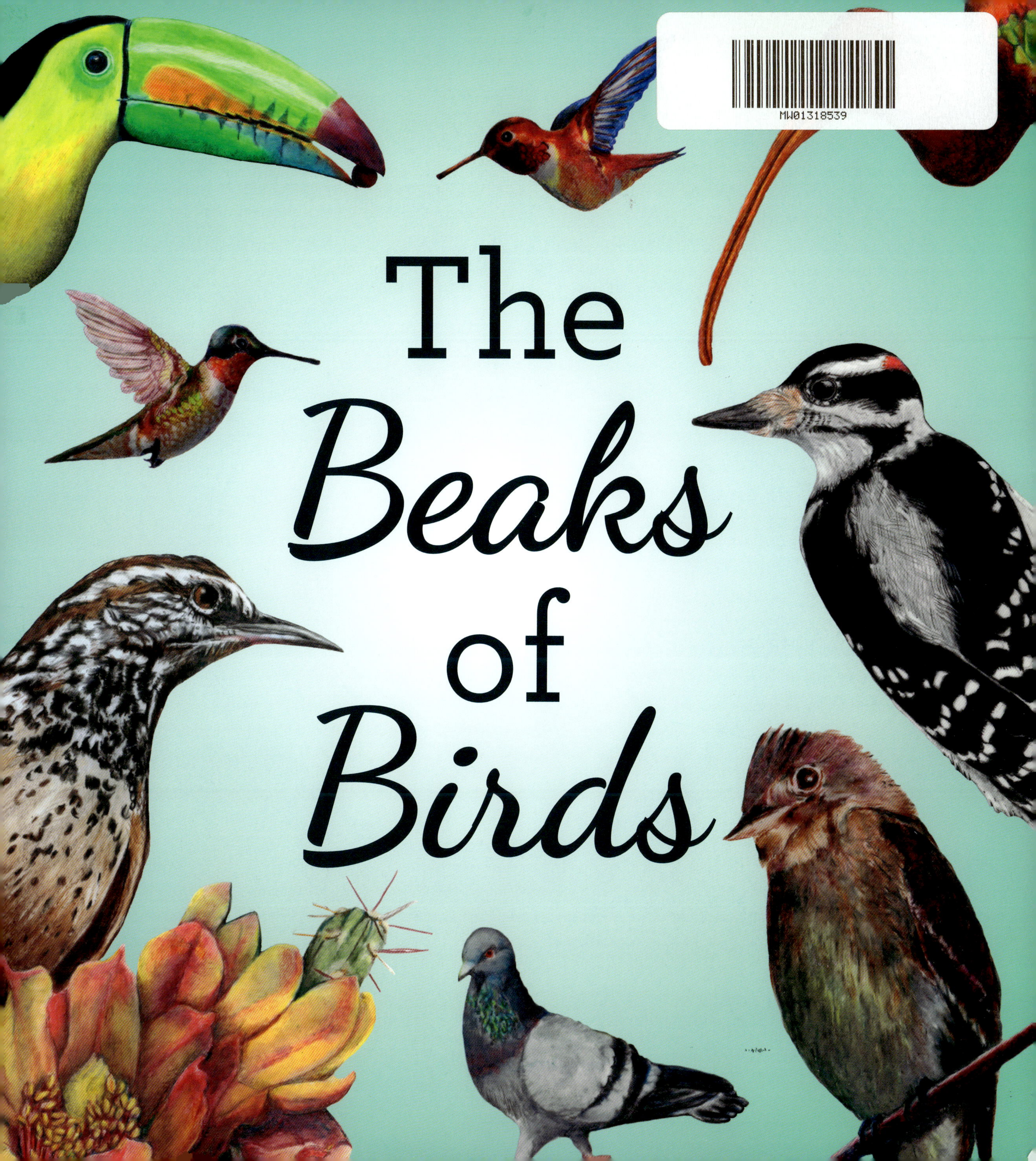
The Beaks of Birds

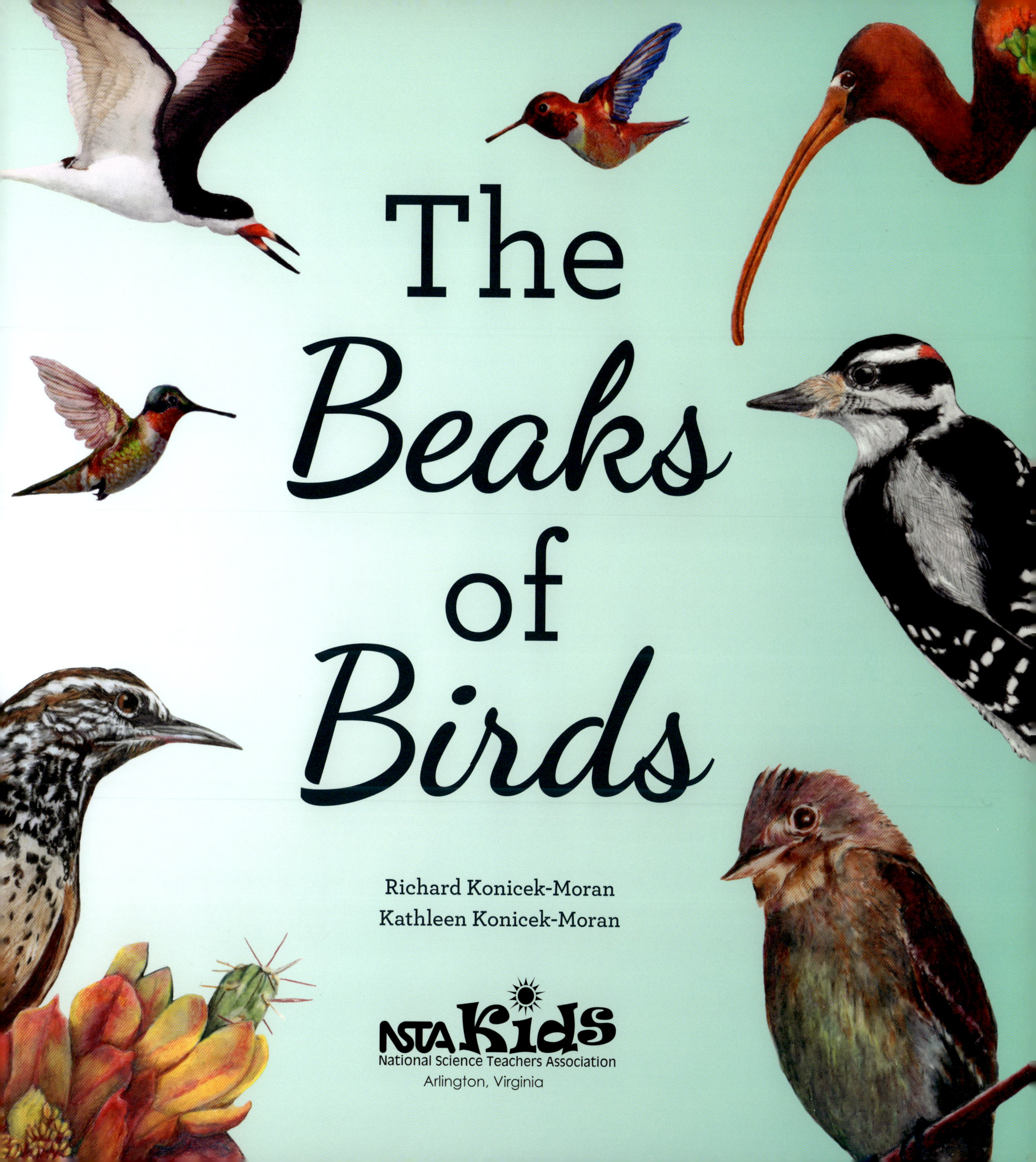

The Beaks of Birds

Richard Konicek-Moran
Kathleen Konicek-Moran

NSTA Kids
National Science Teachers Association
Arlington, Virginia

Claire Reinburg, Director
Rachel Ledbetter, Managing Editor
Deborah Siegel, Associate Editor
Andrea Silen, Associate Editor
Donna Yudkin, Book Acquisitions Manager

ART AND DESIGN
Will Thomas Jr., Director
Himabindu Bichali, Cover, Interior Design
Original illustrations by Kathleen Konicek-Moran

PRINTING AND PRODUCTION
Catherine Lorrain, Director

NATIONAL SCIENCE TEACHERS ASSOCIATION
David L. Evans, Executive Director

1840 Wilson Blvd., Arlington, VA 22201
www.nsta.org/store
For customer service inquiries, please call 800-277-5300.

Lexile® measure: 670L

22 21 20 19 4 3 2 1

NSTA is committed to publishing material that promotes the best in inquiry-based science education. However, conditions of actual use may vary, and the safety procedures and practices described in this book are intended to serve only as a guide. Additional precautionary measures may be required. NSTA and the authors do not warrant or represent that the procedures and practices in this book meet any safety code or standard of federal, state, or local regulations. NSTA and the authors disclaim any liability for personal injury or damage to property arising out of or relating to the use of this book, including any of the recommendations, instructions, or materials contained therein.

Special thanks to Derek Stoner for providing the photograph on which the illustration of the Glossy Ibis (p. 23) is based.

Library of Congress Cataloging-in-Publication Data
Names: Konicek-Moran, Richard, author.
Title: The beaks of birds / by Richard Konicek-Moran and Kathleen Konicek-Moran.
Description: Arlington, VA : National Science Teachers Association, [2018] | Audience: Grade 3 to Grade 5.
Identifiers: LCCN 2018024917 (print) | LCCN 2018026049 (ebook) | ISBN 9781681403564 (e-book) | ISBN 9781681403526 (print)
Subjects: LCSH: Bill (Anatomy)--Juvenile literature.
Classification: LCC QL697 (ebook) | LCC QL697 .K68 2018 (print) | DDC 598.247--dc23
LC record available at https://lccn.loc.gov/2018024917

About This Book

Come with us to explore the wonderful world of birds and their beaks. We will travel from a backyard to a park with a pond to see amazing birds using their beaks—or built-in, specialized "tools"—to eat. Birds use their beaks to do a lot of things: build nests, preen themselves to activate oil glands and keep feathers in proper order, and in some cases defend themselves. In this book, we will concentrate on how birds use their beaks to eat. You may notice that we use the words *beaks* and *bills* in this story. They mean the same thing. "Birders" (people who spend a lot of time looking at birds as a hobby) use both words when they talk about that part of a bird's body.

In this book, we help you understand that the structure of the bird's beak plays a big role in the way birds function to find and capture their food. Engineers call this concept *structure and function* and use it to create many tools that are useful for humans. We call this a *crosscutting concept* because sometimes what we learn in one area of science can be used in others. For example, a paper clip or a thumbtack has certain uses because of its structure, and the way it is used (or functions) depends a lot on its structure or how it is put together. If you look in a toolbox, you can see how screwdrivers, pliers, and other tools are made to perform certain tasks. Applying the concept of structure and function to your toys will help you find out how they work.

To think about structure and function a little more, consider your hands. Your fingers and thumb allow you to grab things that other animals cannot. Think about how you would hold a hammer if you didn't have a thumb. If you have a dog or cat, try to imagine it holding a hammer—it can't, right? Its paws do not have the right structure to hold a hammer.

In the same way, birds need the right type of beak to perform specific tasks. Imagine a woodpecker with a tiny beak. No way could a little beak peck holes in a tree to find bugs to eat. So over millions of years, the woodpecker has developed a beak that is long, sharp, and strong. The same is true for the tools we use when we eat. Over time, people invented the tools they needed for eating different kinds of foods. As you look at the various birds and their bills in this book, think about how they would eat if their beaks were different.

Now read on as you follow your neighbors Mrs. Aiko and Mr. Pedro around as they help you look at the birds in their yard, in the park, and in their photo album. As you look at each bird, think about how their beaks help them survive.

Imagine you like to go walking with your neighbors because they know so much about nature. Both used to be teachers, and they are friends of your family. Mr. and Mrs. Hernandez (you call them Mr. Pedro and Mrs. Aiko) live in an apartment building next door to yours. They have a small yard with bird feeders and have given you a book to write down things you find out in nature. They call it a *field notebook*. Every time you go on a walk with them, you take your field notebook with you, so you can write down the things you see. They often take binoculars with them on their walks to look at birds. Binoculars help make things far away appear closer.

One day, you see Mr. Pedro and Mrs. Aiko excited about something they are looking at through their binoculars. You hurry over to them and learn that they are looking at the first hummingbirds of the season! They put down their binoculars and invite you to go on a walk with them to see what other birds are out today.

"I think a good place to start our walk is at the big bird feeder," suggests Mrs. Aiko. "We have a challenge for you today: Can you tell what each bird eats by the shape of its beak? The shape, or *structure* of the bird's bill has been formed over many, perhaps thousands, of years to have a specific *function,* or way to eat a particular food."

"Look at the bird on the feeder. It's called a House Finch. And underneath the feeder, eating the seeds that the House Finch spills, are little brown birds called House Sparrows. Can you tell what their beaks have in common? What are they eating?" she asks.

"They're eating sunflower seeds!" you say. "Those seeds have a hard cover. I can't eat them without cracking them with my teeth or using a nutcracker. How can those little birds eat them?"

Mrs. Aiko is delighted. "That's exactly right! They do need something like a nutcracker. That's why their bills are big and cone-shaped." Mrs. Aiko takes out a nutcracker to demonstrate how it cracks a walnut. She shows you how the nutcracker has a place to hold the seeds. When you look closely with binoculars at the House Finch, you can see that there is a little bump on the inside of the bill where the bird can hold a seed. You draw a picture in your field notebook of the House Finch's beak and the nutcracker.

HOUSE FINCH (above)
HOUSE SPARROWS (left)

RUBY-THROATED HUMMINGBIRD (left)
ANNA'S HUMMINGBIRD (right)

Mr. Pedro points to a different bird feeder. It does not have seeds, but it has some sort of liquid in it. “Oh, look!” he exclaims. “There’s another hummingbird.”

You look at the tiny bird. The hummingbird pokes its beak into something that looks like a tiny flower on the feeder.

“Its long beak looks like a straw!” you exclaim. “Is it drinking the stuff in the feeder?” you ask.

Mr. Pedro laughs. “You’ve got the right idea! Its long tongue laps up the nectar that is hidden deep down in the flowers. Look! There’s one that’s eating from a flower over there!” He points to another tiny bird darting among the flowers in the garden. “See how it dips its beak in? It needs a long, thin beak to get into very small spaces, just like you need to use something long and thin like a straw to drink from the tiny opening in a bottle. Except you don’t have the right kind of tongue to lap all the way through the straw!”

You spot a bird hopping up the trunk of a tree. Every once in a while, the bird stops and pecks at the trunk, causing bits of bark to fly out from around its beak.

Mrs. Aiko says, "I bet you can guess the name of this bird by just watching what it is doing."

"Pecking bark?" you ask doubtfully, and then you break out in a smile. "Oh, I know! It's a woodpecker!" You look at it more carefully. "It sure does have a strong-looking beak. Why is it pecking, anyway?"

"It has to poke holes in the tree to get bugs that live there," she explains. "Sometimes it has to peck out a big hole in the wood to build a nest for its babies. How do you think the shape of its beak helps it do that?"

You look through your binoculars at the bird. "Its beak looks like a nail that could be hammered into the tree," you answer. "But doesn't it get a headache?"

Mr. Pedro and Mrs. Aiko look at each other and smile. "No, but that's a good question. A woodpecker's skull has a built-in cushion for its brain," says Mr. Pedro.

HAIRY WOODPECKER

Suddenly, you shout, “Oh look! There’s another bird! It just flew out of the bush and ate a fly right out of the air.”

“Interesting!” says Mr. Pedro. “So what would you name that bird?”

You think for a minute. “Insect catcher?” you suggest.

Mr. Pedro looks impressed and tells you that bird is a flycatcher and that it does eat insects.

“Next time it flies, look at its beak,” he suggests.

You wait until it flies out again.

“Its beak is really little!” you say. “Does that make it easy for the flycatcher to snatch insects out of the air?”

Mr. Pedro nods his head. “Some flycatchers even have a little hook on their beak so that they can hold onto the insect better.”

You look at a tree nearby. "Oh, wow!" you say. "Look at that funny bird coming down the tree head first."

"Yes," says Mr. Pedro, "that's a nuthatch, and its beak is shaped just right for prying under the bark. Can you see it?"

You look as carefully as you can. The nuthatch's bill seems to be tilted upward. You can imagine it lifting up bark with its beak.

"Sometimes," Mr. Pedro explains, "it actually puts a seed into a crack in the bark and 'hacks' at it to get the good stuff inside. Maybe that's why we call it a nuthatch, because 'hack' sounded like 'hatch' to the people who named the bird long ago."

GREAT BLUE HERON

"Let's go to the park and see what birds are hanging around the pond," says Mrs. Aiko.

At the park, you see a huge bird that is about 4 feet tall and stands very still in the pond as it looks into the water. "What is that bird?" you ask.

"That's a Great Blue Heron," responds Mrs. Aiko. "How would you describe its beak?"

"It's long and pointy, like a dagger or knife. Is it waiting to spear a big fish with that long, sharp beak?"

"Yay!" Mr. Pedro cheers. "You figured that one out quickly. Herons don't always spear their prey. Most of the time they catch fish between their upper and lower beaks, but every once in a while they stab through the fish or other critter, just like our ancestors who hunted. See how it just stands there, looking into the pond?"

Suddenly, the big bird's head and neck dart into the water. The heron comes up with a fish in its beak. It flips the bird into the air to swallow it whole, headfirst.

"Hey! Look at that bird in the pond. All I see is its bottom!" you exclaim.

"Yes, it is doing what scientists call 'dabbling.' It kind of tips over in the water and scoops up anything it touches. Some ducks do that. Look at its bill when it comes back up," says Mrs. Aiko. "The bill is broad and has a way of filtering out things it doesn't want to eat. This bird is a Mallard and is found in most of North America. It eats anything its bill can reach, such as plants or even insects or worms. It even has a little tooth-like knob on the end so it can pick up insects and worms when it feeds on dry land."

Mr. Pedro shows you a picture of the Mallard's bill up close on his cell phone. You copy that picture into your field notebook.

"We have some pictures on our phone that we took on our trips to Florida, Arizona, and the local zoo," says Mr. Pedro. "You'll see some beaks that will knock your socks off!"

MALLARD

As they flip through the photos from their trip to Florida, you see a bird that excites you and yell, "Stop!" The bird is big and black and white, and it has a long, curved bill and pink feet.

"That's a long beak. I bet it spears lots of big fish," you say.

"Actually, it doesn't strike its prey like the heron. It eats just about anything it catches in the mud and has a completely different way of hunting. This bird is called a Wood Stork, and it is the only type of stork in North America. What do you notice about its head?"

"It's bald! Why doesn't it have feathers on its head?" you ask.

"Great question! The Wood Stork puts its open beak into the water and swishes it back and forth until something touches it. Then, it snaps its beak shut on its prey. It's a good thing that the Wood Stork evolved over millions of years to be bald, or else the feathers on its head would get muddy," replies Mrs. Aiko.

"Oh, here's a pretty bird. But its beak is weird," you say, as you examine the picture closely. "It looks like the lower part of the beak is longer than the top."

"That's a Black Skimmer," answers Mr. Pedro. "Does that name give you a clue about how it feeds?"

"It looks like it's flying very close to the water. Is it using its beak as a scoop?"

"Well, sort of," replies Mrs. Aiko. "As it flies over the ocean, it dips the bottom half of its beak in and 'skims' a fish or two into its bill. It looks for schools of fish that swim close to the surface."

"That's amazing," you say. "I'd really like to see that bird up close."

"Now here is a picture of a bird that has an unusual beak. See how it curves. It has just the right bill for poking around in holes in the water, grass, or mud to catch a bug or small reptile," says Mrs. Aiko.

"What's it called?" you ask.

"An ibis," replies Mr. Pedro. "They come in two colors: white and a glossy dark color. The ancient Egyptians used to worship its relative, the Sacred Ibis, as the god Thoth and even buried it with mummies."

Mrs. Aiko adds, "This picture of the Glossy Ibis is very special because we usually think of these birds as being black. But at certain times of the year and in just the right light, you can see all the beautiful colors, what scientists call *iridescence,* which can be found in their feathers."

"Oh my goodness! Look at this beautiful pink bird with the strange beak. It looks like it has a scoop at the end."

"Why don't you give naming this bird a try," says Mr. Pedro.

You look closely at the picture. The beak is shaped like a spoon.

"Spoonbeak?" you say.

"You're on the right track! That's a Roseate Spoonbill. Another clever name, right? The spoonbill swings its beak in the water, and the shape of it lifts the water and all the little critters in there up into the beak," explains Mr. Pedro. "There are little filtering, teeth-like knobs on the beak that help the bird keep its prey but then let the water swish right out."

You make sure to include a sketch of the spoonbill's beak in your field notebook. Its head is bald, too, for the same reason as the Wood Stork.

"I know this bird. It's a pelican," you say.

"We saw these everywhere along the water in Florida," comments Mr. Pedro.

"There's a silly poem by an old-time author named Dixon Lanier Merritt that goes along with this bird. 'A wonderful bird is a pelican. Its bill can hold more than its belly can,'" Mrs. Aiko tells you.

"Look at the size of that beak!" you exclaim. "I bet it catches really big fish."

"Well, you would think so, but actually it crashes into the water from high above and stuns *little* fish. Then, it scoops them up into its huge throat pouch," Mrs. Aiko explains.

"A big fish with big bones can cause harm if it gets stuck in a pelican's throat," says Mr. Pedro. "So as it flies away, the pelican drains the water out of its pouch. Sometimes, gulls try to steal fish out of its beak while it is flying. And a pelican is so big that a gull may actually perch on its head to do its stealing!"

"Is that a fish in the pelican's beak?" you wonder.

"What do you think?" Mrs. Aiko asks.

BROWN PELICAN

KEEL-BILLED TOUCAN

Oh, boy! I have never seen anything like this bird. Did you take this picture at the zoo?" you ask.

"Yes," responds Mrs. Aiko. "You would have to go to Central or South America to see a toucan in the wild. It lives only in the tropics."

"That beak is so huge. I bet it can eat anything," you say.

"It eats fruit and some other things, including small critters. You can see that this one is eating something called a palm fruit," says Mrs. Aiko.

"How can it hold its head up with a beak that big?" you ask.

"Its beak is large but actually very light," explains Mr. Pedro, "and underneath the covering of the toucan's beak are lots of blood vessels so that it can cool itself off in warm weather and warm itself up in cool weather. Isn't that amazing? Remember when we started this walk, we talked about how a bird's beak is structured to help the bird eat specific foods? Well, this heating and cooling ability is another example of how structure helps the bird function better."

"This bird sitting on a cactus must be from the desert, right? It has a long, curved beak. Does that make it easier for it to poke deeply into the cactus and get bugs?" you ask.

"Yes, it's from the southwest desert, where we found it on our trip to Phoenix, Arizona. And, yes, the big beak does help. This bird—the Cactus Wren—lives in the desert where it is hard for it to find much to eat except bugs. Snakes are too big for this little guy," explains Mrs. Aiko. "An amazing fact about this desert dweller is that it doesn't drink water. It gets water only from what it eats!"

You think about this fact for a little while. "I guess that makes sense," you respond. "Deserts don't have much water, but somehow these Cactus Wrens have found a way to survive."

CACTUS WREN

As you all get ready to leave the park, you notice another bird. It is sitting high up on a post and looking down all around. You take a closer look at the bird's beak through your binoculars.

"That looks like a really sharp, hooked beak!" you say. "Is that beak meant for tearing things apart?"

"It is!" says Mr. Pedro. "This bird is an American Kestrel, and it has lots of relatives with the same kind of beak, such as ospreys, hawks, eagles, and owls. They are called birds of prey or raptors."

"I don't know if you've ever watched anybody in your family getting meat ready to be cooked," Mrs. Aiko adds, "but it takes a very sharp instrument to cut through skin to get to the meat. Birds of prey kill their targets with their feet and then take them back to a branch or nest, and use their spiked bills to eat."

It's dinnertime so you have to go home. You thank your neighbors for taking you on their bird walk. While you are heading home, you see some pigeons on a fountain and wonder what kind of bills they have and how their bills help them eat. You ask yourself, "What do pigeons eat, anyway?" You write this question down in your field notebook.

As you turn onto your street, you think about all the beaks you have seen today and how they relate to what birds eat. You don't like the thought of eating bugs and frogs like some birds. Then, you think about your own mouth. You have teeth for biting and teeth for grinding. Your mouth is perfect for what you eat, and you are happy to be just what you are.

Activities

1. Look inside a toolbox or visit a hardware store and examine the various tools. Can you tell what each tool is used for by its shape?

2. Go to the kitchen and look at the tools used there, such as a spatula. How does its shape help it do the job it was designed for?

3. Is there a tool that you would like to have for something you want to do? Draw a tool that does a particular job because of its structure.

4. Try picking up bits of yarn with a clothespin, red liquid with an eye dropper, or raisins out of a cookie using various "beaks" (or tools such spoons or tweezers). Which tool worked the best? What about that tool's design made it work the best?

5. Look at some other life forms, such as plants or insects, and see how their structure helps them function better. For instance, how do you think the thorns on a rose help the plant survive? How do the giant eyes of dragonflies work to protect them?

6. Go out to a local park and look at birds. Take a field notebook and record what birds you see. Sketch them, and make notes about what they do. Look at the feet of birds. Can you see how their shape helps the birds in some way? Download different birding apps such as eBird and Merlin on your cell phone to help you identify the birds.

7. Put up a bird feeder in your backyard and keep track of what birds come to it during different parts of the year and what they like to eat.

8. Look for an organization that helps protect birds. The National Audubon Society may have a chapter near you. Visit the organization's office and see if it has books and pamphlets you can read to tell you more about birds. See if there are things you can do to help, such as going on a Hawk Watch or on a Christmas Bird Count.

Background Information for Parents and Teachers

Until 1851, not much was known about the origin of birds. Only then were fossils found that gave clues about the ancestors of birds. The current theory is that birds are descended from dinosaurs because fossils of dinosaurs have been found with feathers. Feathers may have been useful to dinosaurs for breeding purposes (color is often important when attracting a mate) or for insulation against cold weather.

Birds are one of the most popular animals for people to study. Birders are found everywhere, armed with binoculars as they try to identify birds in the wild. They contribute greatly to scientific knowledge, such as the National Audubon Society volunteers who count migrating hawks during the annual Hawk Watch or participate in the Christmas Bird Count. These two counts are important to help determine population levels of bird species around the world. Bird tourism is a great aid to local economies and is especially important in developing countries to help preserve the environment. There are a number of contests that award prizes to people who have the longest list of birds sighted in a certain state or country or even worldwide. The contests are great for promoting bird tourism.

In this book, we focus on the *beaks* or *bills* of birds (the terms are interchangeable) as an indicator of structure and function. Over millions of years, birds' beaks have evolved into different shapes, which give us clues about how a specific bird uses its beak to find food. Beaks are bony underneath and are covered with keratin, a substance that is also found in human hair and fingernails.

In this story, we see a child and his or her neighbors observe birds and consider how their beaks determine what they eat, but we could do the same by examining our own way of eating. For example, you choose a soup spoon to eat soup because it is shaped to bring the soup from the bowl to your mouth. It has a wider head than a regular spoon and thus is more capable of bringing liquid to your mouth without spilling. Humans designed spoons to do this, but, in nature, it is the effects of the environment on animals that eventually create changes in animal forms. Animals with adaptations that are useful for surviving in a specific environment are more successful than others in their species who have not adapted. Thus, the successful animals live to have offspring, and the adaptation is carried on.

Charles Darwin completed a five-year voyage in 1836 and began to wonder about the differences he saw in the birds he had collected—especially the beaks. First, the mockingbirds that varied from island to island intrigued him. Later, he examined the finches he had collected and found that similar birds from different islands had differently shaped beaks. He formulated a question as to how this variation could have occurred. Years later, when he published his groundbreaking book *On the Origin of Species* (1859), he still had no knowledge of genetics, but he proposed a theory that species were formed in their struggle to survive changes in their environment. He theorized that millions of years ago, small starling-like birds were blown from the shores of Ecuador 500 miles west to the Galapagos Islands. Because they were isolated from other birds of their kind, they evolved into the unique birds that live there now.

In 1973, a husband-and-wife team from Princeton University, professors Peter and Rosemary Grant, began a study on the Galapagos Islands that would last four decades. By observing many, many generations of birds on an uninhabited volcanic outcropping called Daphne Major, they discovered that drought and deluge affected the form and size of the beaks of finches that lived on the island from year to year. When drought hit the island and food was scarce, most finches with beaks too small to crack seeds died. However, the birds with large, strong beaks survived and thrived. When there was plenty of water and the plant life flourished, birds with smaller beaks did survive (Weiner 1994).

Scientists have determined that there are now 14 different species of finches on the Galapagos Islands. Actually, these birds are not true finches. They are in the tanager family but are still called *Darwin's finches*. Later, scientists were able to identify the gene responsible for determining beak shape, and then they discovered that drought and deluge affected the form and size of the beaks of the surviving finches. The story of Darwin's finches reminds us that cause and effect, like structure and function, is a concept that applies to what happens in nature.

References

Darwin, C. 1859. *On the origin of species by means of natural selection, or preservation of favored races in the struggle for life.* London: John Murray.

Weiner, J. 1994. *The beak of the finch: A story of evolution in our time.* New York: Random House.